Thesaurus Rex

Written by Laya Steinberg
Illustrated by Debbie Harter

Barefoot Books
Celebrating Art and Story

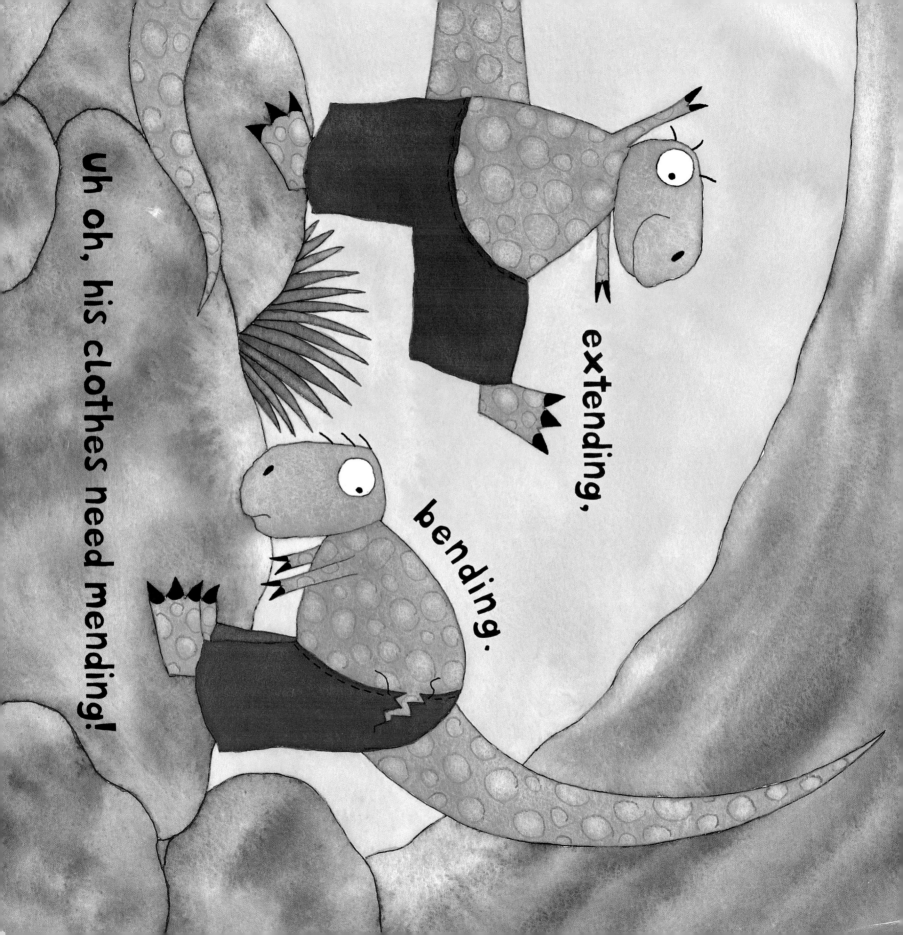

uh oh, his clothes need mending!

extending.

bending.

Thesaurus Rex drinks his milk:
sip, sup, swallow, swill.

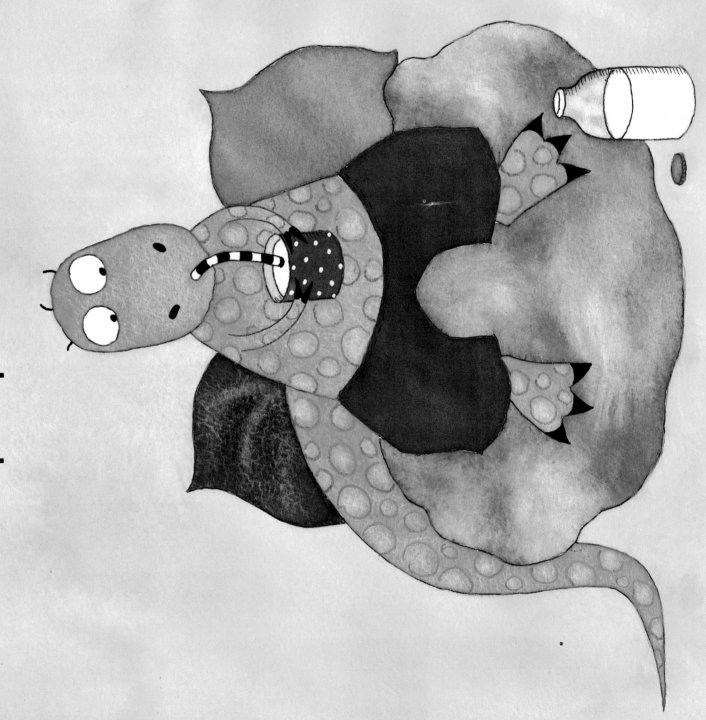

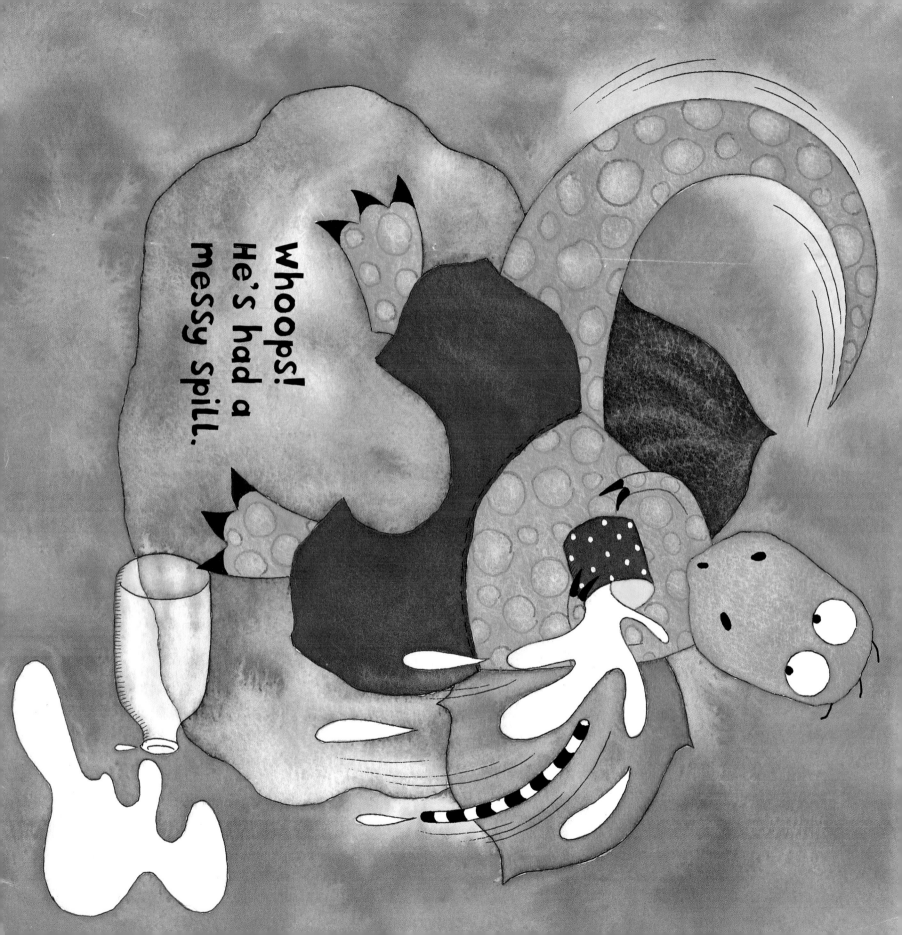

Thesaurus Rex goes exploring:

hunting,

searching,

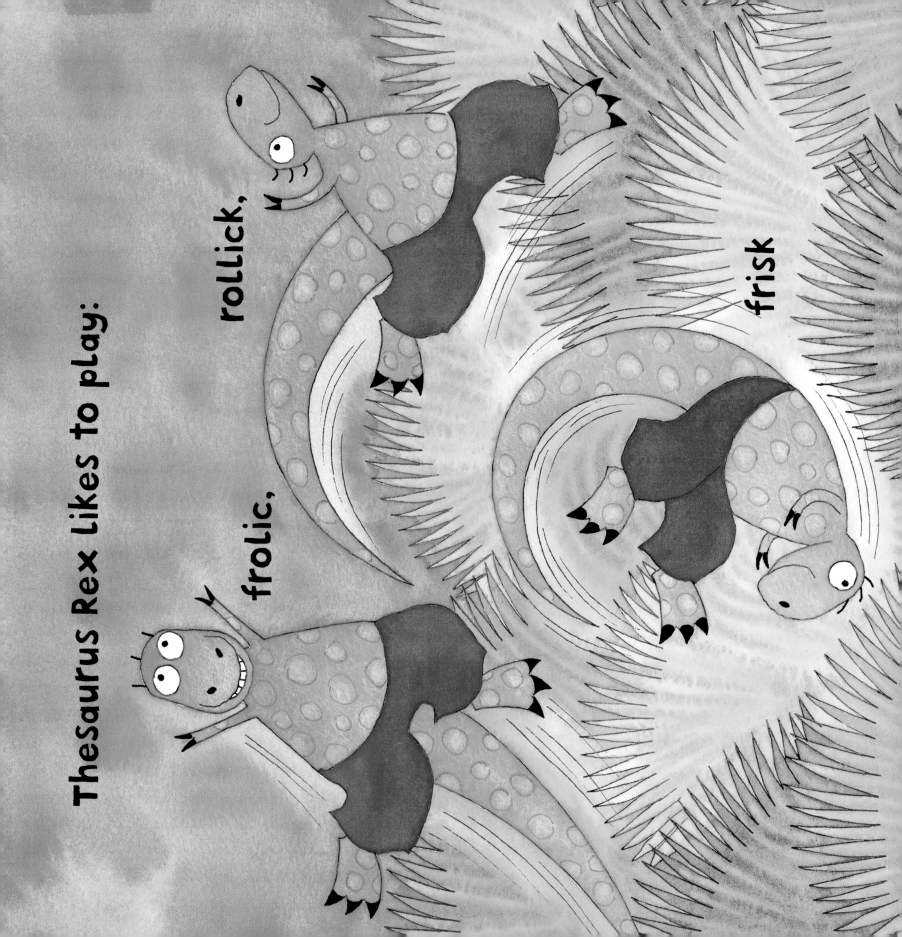

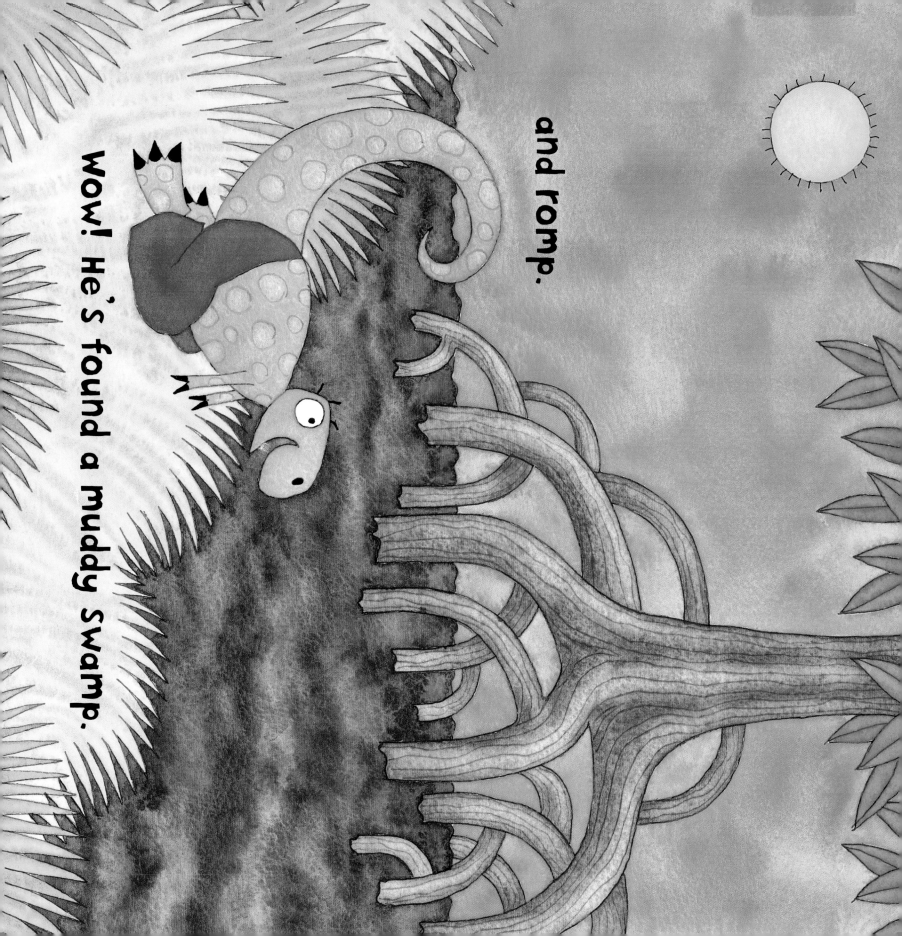

slide

and glide.

Whee! What a speedy ride!

Thesaurus Rex lands in mud:
slime, slush, mire and muck.

Thesaurus Rex must get clean:

wash,

bathe,

Scour

and scrub.

He's left footprints
in the tub.

TheSaurus Rex is ready to eat:
munch, crunch, nibble, gnaw.

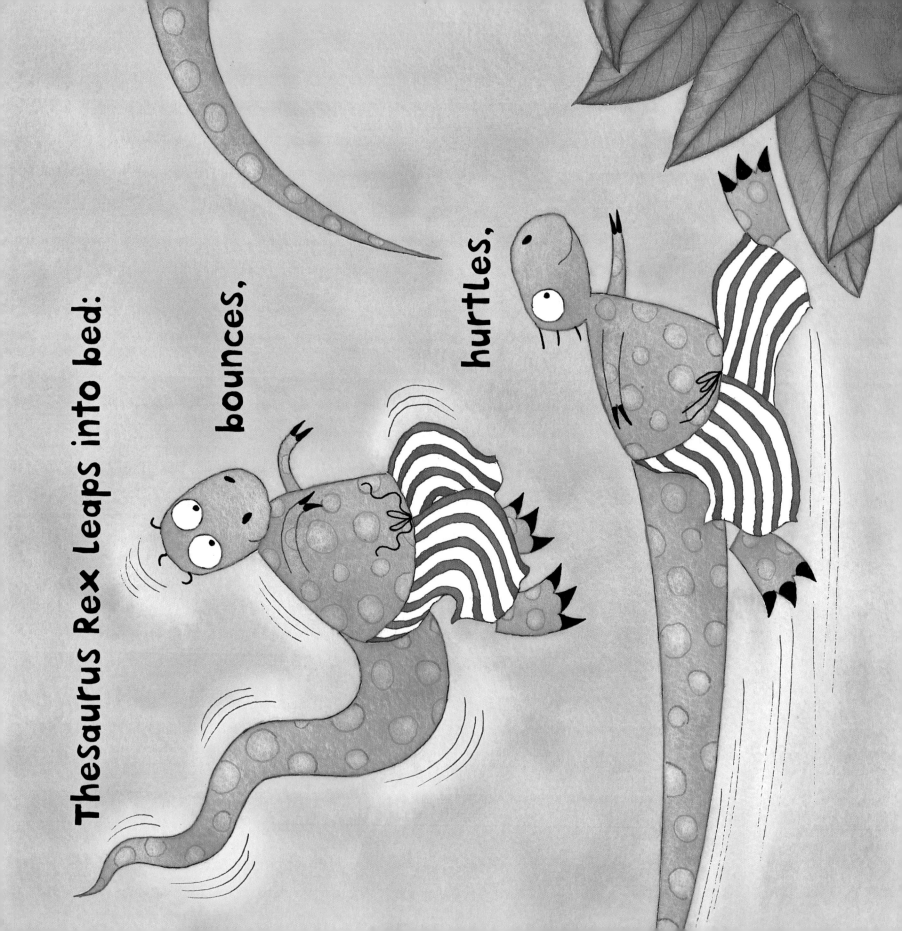

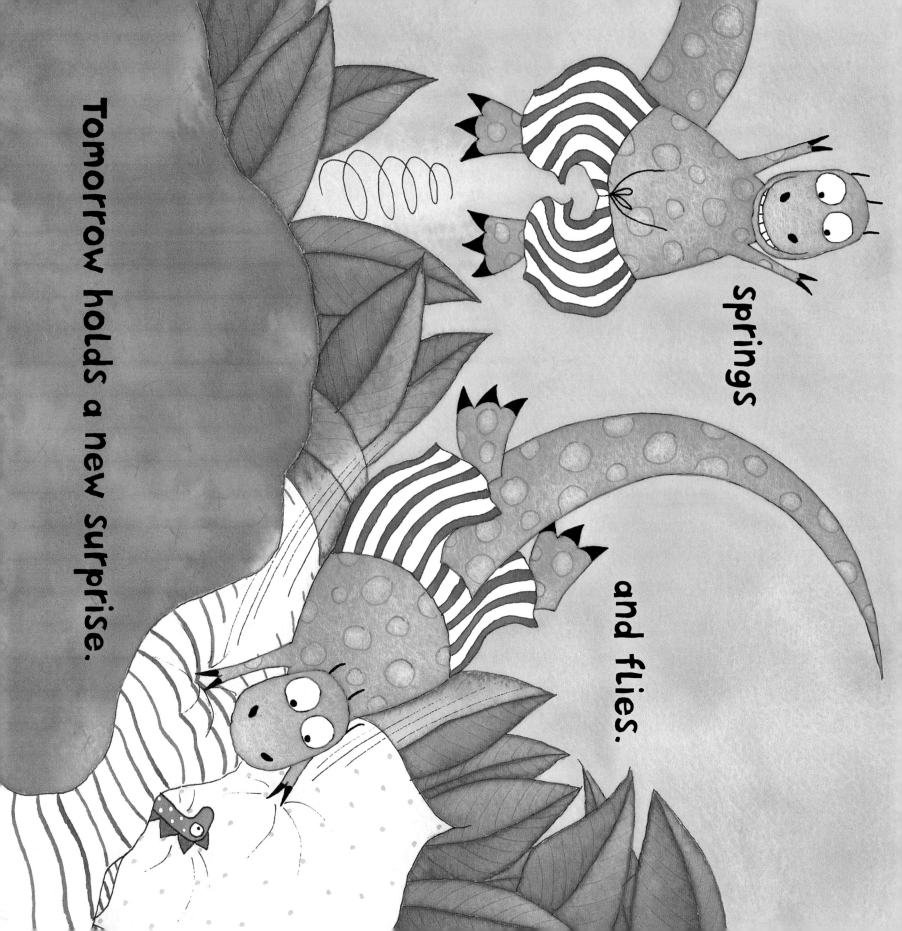

Tomorrow holds a new surprise.

springs

and flies.

Thesaurus Rex is all wrapped up:
bundled,
covered,
tucked in tight.

He'll have happy dreams tonight. Goodnight!

Barefoot Books
124 Walcot Street
Bath
BA1 5BG

This book was typeset in Bokka.
The illustrations were prepared in watercolour,
pen and ink and crayon on thick watercolour paper

Graphic design by Big Blu Ltd.
Colour separation by Grafiscan, Verona
Printed and bound in Hong Kong by South China Printing co.

This book has been printed on 100% acid-free paper

1 3 5 7 9 8 6 4 2

Hardback ISBN 1-84148-054-1

Barefoot Books
Celebrating Art and Story

At Barefoot Books, we celebrate art and story with books that open the hearts and minds of children from all walks of life, inspiring them to read deeper, search further, and explore their own creative gifts. Taking our inspiration from many different cultures, we focus on themes that encourage independence of spirit, enthusiasm for learning, and acceptance of other traditions. Thoughtfully prepared by writers, artists and storytellers from all over the world, our products combine the best of the present with the best of the past to educate our children as the caretakers of tomorrow.

www.barefootbooks.com